The
Adirondack
Kids®#10

The Final Daze of Summer

The Adirondack Kids® #10

The Final Daze of Summer

By Justin & Gary VanRiper
Illustrations by Carol VanRiper

Adirondack Kids Press, Ltd.
Camden, New York

The Adirondack Kids® #10
The Final Daze of Summer

Justin & Gary VanRiper
Copyright © 2010. All rights reserved.

First Paperback Edition, May 2010

Cover illustration by Susan Loeffler
Illustrated by Carol McCurn VanRiper

Published by
Adirondack Kids Press, Ltd.
39 Second Street
Camden, New York 13316
www.adirondackkids.com

Printed in the United States of America
by Patterson Printing, Michigan

ISBN 978-0-9826250-0-2

Other Books
by Justin and Gary VanRiper

The Adirondack Kids®

The Adirondack Kids® #2
Rescue on Bald Mountain

The Adirondack Kids® #3
The Lost Lighthouse

The Adirondack Kids® #4
The Great Train Robbery

The Adirondack Kids® #5
Islands in the Sky

The Adirondack Kids® #6
Secret of the Skeleton Key

The Adirondack Kids® #7
Mystery of the Missing Moose

The Adirondack Kids® #8
Escape from Black Bear Mountain

The Adirondack Kids® #9
Legend of the Lake Monster

Other Books
by Justin VanRiper

The Adirondack Kids® Story & Coloring Book
Runaway Dax

During this, the 10th anniversary
of *The Adirondack Kids*®, we thank our
loyal readers who have grown
with us and supported us and our
work throughout the decade!

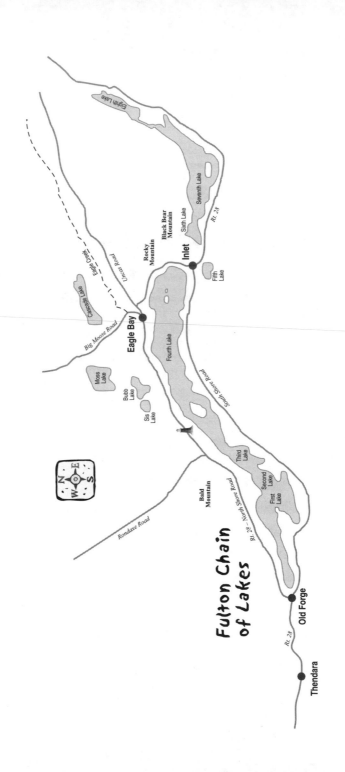

Contents

"Wait until I put my thumb up!"
Justin Robert said.

Chapter One

Justin Attempts
a Laker

"Wait until I put my thumb up," Justin Robert called over the sound of the family motor boat, the *Tamarack*, its engine idling in the waters of Fourth Lake. He trusted his best friend, Jackie Salsberry, to be his spotter.

His other best friend, Nick Barnes, was also in the boat, but far too often he got the hand signals confused and gave the driver poor instructions.

Earlier that summer, Justin signaled for the boat to wait and Nick thought he meant to gun it. The boat took off and Justin wasn't ready. The rope went taut and the sudden jolt made his arms feel like they were coming out of their sockets! He was so sore he couldn't swim or cast a fishing line for days. Nick was a great friend, just not a very good spotter. His job on this ride? Keep a watchful eye on his calico cat, Dax.

Jackie pulled her long, blonde hair back into a pony tail so it wouldn't toss and tangle in the wind that would be created by the speeding boat. She called back to Justin, "Are you almost ready?"

Sitting on the edge of the family dock, Justin had already slipped his feet into the black rubber boots of the wakeboard and holding on to the long yellow tow rope, jumped in with a splash. He loved this sport. It reminded him of skateboarding, except it was a lot faster! A red maple leaf carrying a damsel fly sailed by his face that was now half submerged in the late-August water which was warmer than the air.

This was it – his last chance before the end of summer vacation to try and make one full lap all the way around the lake's perimeter without wiping out. The Labor Day crowds had not yet arrived to churn the water with their final boat rides of the season, and the calm face of the lake this early morning shone like glass.

Justin positioned his body as if he was seated in a rocking chair. He tipped his head back and took a deep breath. "Okay!" he shouted, and pointed his thumb at the sunny Adirondack sky.

Jackie relayed the signal to Justin's mom at the wheel of the *Tamarack*. The engine gunned and the rope tightened. Justin leaned his weight onto his right leg and slightly turned his hips. Maintaining a firm grip on the rope, he was pulled forward through the water and suddenly popped to the surface.

Justin couldn't hear her, but he could tell from Jackie's expression and upraised hands that she was cheering. It was a perfect start, but what he didn't know was whether or not he had the strength to endure the entire fourteen miles in the forty-five minutes that it would take to complete his very first laker!

Chapter Two

"Duck! It's a Flamingo!"

Justin knew his mom and dad didn't think he could make it all the way around the lake without a break, but what he appreciated was that as long as he set goals for himself in activities that weren't dangerous, they always supported him and encouraged him to try.

Already around Eagle Bay and passing Gull Rock, it was the farthest he had ever made it without losing his balance. He had drifted asleep the night before, imagining his strategy for the historic lap. It was simple. He wouldn't try anything fancy and would just hold on for dear life! If he did pass his friend, Captain Conall McBride, riding by in his mail boat, or race by a load of passengers on the cruise boat, he would not let go to wave even for a split second!

Jackie pointed to a spot off to his left.

Justin felt his stomach tighten. *Trouble?* he thought. *A rock? A swimmer? Another boat?* He had no plans to swerve from directly behind the *Tamarack* to spray water through the air. That would take too much energy and be way too risky.

What a relief it was to pass from a safe distance

two common loons – their white-checkered black backs easily seen rising and falling on their boat's rolling waves. Justin smiled. *Probably the same loons we saved from those mean jet skiers at the beginning of the summer,* he thought.*

Justin's heart pounded faster. Alger Island was in view now. That meant he would soon be racing past the Shoal Point Lighthouse.

While his fingers gripping the handle of the tow rope were beginning to ache a little, he ignored the pain. Instead, he concentrated on a vision of himself letting go of the rope to glide across the last few feet of water in front of a dock full of cheering family and friends. And there he would be – bobbing in his life jacket before them all, in victory.

Speeding past the lighthouse and making the wide turn around the end of the island, this time it was Nick who began pointing at something. Justin wasn't sure, but it appeared as if his friend was also repeating a particular word over and over.

Duck? Justin thought. *What duck? First loons, and now a duck?* He was not amused. *We're almost half-way done, Nick Barnes. You had better not make me start laughing and fall down!*

Nick was holding Dax, but deciding to point using both hands, he dropped the calico to the floor of the boat, which sent Jackie scrambling to pick her up.

And that was when Justin noticed it – a massive winged shadow in the foamy water right beside him. It was now clear what Nick was so excited about;

6

a creature was flying somewhere over his head. His first thought was to take his friend's advice and duck. Both terrified and angry, he tried instead to steal a quick glance at his mysterious pursuer. And that was when he, like the creature above him, became airborne, and his quest for a laker ended with a spectacular, *Ka-Splash*.

It was a wet and bewildered wakeboard warrior who suddenly found himself heading back to camp wrapped in a beach towel on the back seat of the *Tamarack* between his two friends, who were arguing loud enough to compete with the engine's roar.

"It was not a flamingo!" Jackie said.

Nick persisted. "Yes, it was!" he said.

"That's impossible," Jackie shot back. "Flamingos don't live in the Adirondacks."

Nick shook his head. "I don't care where the creepy birds live," he said. "I know what I saw – and I saw a flamingo!"

* see *The Adirondack Kids® #1*

7

Chapter Three

"Do You Have Any Black Fly Pies?"

Justin pleaded. "Can we just play the game now?" He was tired of hearing his friend describe in detail his untimely crash in the lake.

Nick kept shaking his head. "It was so weird seeing you flying upside down in the air like that," he said. "I thought for sure you were doomed."

"I vote with Justin that we play the game," Jackie said. She led them down the grassy hill to the edge of the lake. "I'll be the bear and Justin can be the shopkeeper."

Nick stopped and groaned. "I don't want to be the pie again," he said. "I want to be the bear."

"Come here, Nick," Justin said. "I've got a flavor Jackie will never guess."

"I get three tries," Jackie said. "If I can't guess what kind of pie you are in three tries, then you can be the bear."

Nick looked at Justin. "Is it a really good flavor?" he said. "One she'll never get?"

Justin nodded. "It's really, really good," he said. "She won't guess it in a million years."

Reluctantly, Nick agreed to be the pie and let Justin whisper into his ear the kind of flavor he would be. The recipe made him beam. "Ha, you'll never guess what kind of pie I am," he said, and took his place behind the small boulder that now became the counter of the Pie Shop.

Justin stood in front of the counter as the shop-keeper, and waited for his first customer.

Jackie stepped forward and opened an invisible door. "Ding-aling-aling," she sang, mimicking the sound of a bell.

"Welcome to the Pie Shop, Mrs. Bear," Justin said. "What kind of pie were you looking for today?"

Jackie growled. "Shopkeeper?" she said, in the deepest bear voice she could muster. "Do you have any *pumpkin* pies today?"

Justin laughed. "No, I'm sorry," he said. "We don't have any *pumpkin* pies today."

Nick smiled.

Jackie growled again. "Shopkeeper?" she asked. "Do you have any *rhubarb* pies today?"

"What's rhubarb?" Nick asked.

"Shhh, pies can't talk," Justin said. He turned to Jackie. "No, I'm sorry, Mrs. Bear, we don't have any *rhubarb* pies."

"Ha, ha," Nick said. "It looks like your little cubby bears are going to starve today!"

Jackie glared at Nick. "Shopkeeper?" she said without hesitation. "Do you have any *black fly* pies today?"

9

Before Justin could answer, Nick squealed and made a dash toward the water pump.

Growling, Jackie took off after him.

Nick yelled as he ran. "No fair, no fair," he said. "Justin said you'd never guess."

"Run, Nick, run!" Justin said, as he watched his friend, the black fly pie, make a sharp turn around the fire pit, knock over an Adirondack chair and disappear behind the lean-to.

Jackie roared and Nick knew she was gaining on him. If he could just make it around the lean-to, he would be back to the boulder that was the counter of the Pie Shop and home free!

Justin easily heard the growling and the screaming that was coming from behind the pine log structure. The pounding of sneakers on the hard ground grew louder, telling him the two were about to come back into view.

When they reappeared, Nick still had a step on Jackie, but Justin could see it was a lost cause. He winced as he watched the bear, still growling, throw her arms around the waist of the black fly pie and drag it kicking and hollering to the ground. In seconds, she had the pie pinned underneath her.

The bear squinted and looked down on the terrified pie. "So – my cubs are going to go hungry tonight?" she said. "I don't think so." She lifted her head and roared in such a way that she scared both the pie and the shopkeeper!

"Let me up, let me up," Nick said. "You win."

Jackie snarled one more time, laughed and stood up. "You're just lucky I don't like black fly pie," she said.

The three friends sat down on the floor of the lean-to facing the lake.

Nick finally caught his breath. "Next time I get to be the bear," he said.

"Speaking of bears," Justin said. "I wonder if we'll be able to sleep out here this weekend and watch the fireworks?"

Jackie shook her head. "Not if the Labor Day Bear is on the prowl again," she said.

Justin folded his arms and grunted in a tone of defiance. "Some weird bird made me lose my last chance for a laker this year," he said. "I'm not letting some dumb old bear take away my last weekend of the summer in the lean-to."

"We won't get to sleep out if our parents say no," Jackie said. "You know bears are nothing to mess around with."

Justin hung his head. "I know," he said.

"It is really too bad that flamingo made you fall down," Nick said. "At least you would have your laker."

Jackie sighed. "Do you want me to pin you on the ground again?" she said. "Leave Justin alone. And how many times do I have to tell you that bird could not have been a flamingo."

Nick frowned at her.

"So what could it have been?" Justin said.

Jackie turned to Nick. "Describe it for me again,

and don't just say it was really big with wings. Think carefully. What exactly did it look like?"

Nick stared out at the lake, as if deep in thought. "Well, the glare from the water was kind of in my eyes," he said.

Jackie sighed. "There wasn't any glare," she said. "The sun was at our back. You should have had a perfect look at it. Tell me about its color or shape or any unusual marks it had."

"It was pretty big, and had a really long beak that was kind of bent on the end – like it flew face first into a wall," Nick said. "I saw birds just like it last winter when we were visiting my grandma and grandpa on vacation down south by the ocean."

"Was the bird pink?" Justin said, "If it was a flamingo, it must have been pink."

Nick blushed. As the interrogation continued, he was becoming less certain about the bird's identity. "I don't think so," he said. "It was more a darkish color."

Jackie shook her head. "I know what bird it was," she said. The boys perked up. "It was a cormorant."

Nick looked puzzled. "A corn-a-what?" he said.

"A double-crested cormorant," Jackie said. "It's the only bird in the Adirondacks that fits. You said it was dark in color and with a long beak that is hooked on the end, right?"

Nick nodded.

Jackie smiled. "Great," she said. "I hope it stays around long enough so I can see it and add it to my 'life list'."

"Your 'life list'," Nick said. "What's that?"

"Isn't it kind of like a diary?" Justin asked.

"Well, kind of," Jackie said. "It's a giant check-list of all the birds in the world. And when you see a bird in the wild for the first time, you check it off the list. During my lifetime I'm going to try to see at least all the different birds in the Adirondacks."

The sound of a boat horn at the dock stirred them into action.

"Hey, look, it's Ranger Bill," Nick said, and turned to Justin. "He must be here to see your mom and dad."

"That's kind of strange," Justin said. "He's usually really busy on Labor Day weekend and doesn't stop anywhere unless it's serious business."

Jackie was already running to greet him.

Chapter Four

A Looney Discovery

"Are you sure?" Mrs. Robert said, handing the ranger a glass of fresh lemonade.

Ranger Bill took a sip and sat back resting the glass on the arm of his Adirondack chair. "Thank you," he said. "Yes, we're positive. Reports have come in now from several very reliable sources confirming the identity of the species."

Justin, Jackie and Nick rushed from the kitchen with their own drinks to join the ranger and Justin's parents out on the camp's front porch.

"Species?" Nick said. "Isn't that like something from outer space? Did people see an alien?" He groaned. "I knew aliens were hiding somewhere in these mountains."

"Be quiet, Nick," Jackie said.

Nick would not be silenced. "Why?" he said. "We'll never get to sleep out in the lean-to if there are aliens out there waiting to grab us."

"We're talking about a species of bird," Mr. Robert said. "A bird that has never before been seen in the Adirondacks."

"So, what is it?" Justin asked. "What bird are people seeing?"

"A Brown Pelican," Ranger Bill said, and took another sip of his lemonade. "It has been observed on several lakes nearby, including up on Tupper, but it's believed to be headed right now toward us here on Fourth Lake."

Nick looked straight at Jackie and began to gloat. "Ha! You thought it was a bubble-crested comb-the-ants," he said.

Jackie corrected him. "Double-crested cormorant," she said. "And you said it was a flamingo!"

Ranger Bill leaned forward. "You've seen the bird?" he said.

Nick loved the attention. "Yes, I did," he said. "It was flying over Justin's head when he was on his wakeboard and came so close to him that it made him wipe out. You should have seen Justin. He was probably upside down in the air for like five whole minutes before he splashed back into the water."

Justin sighed. Not only was he tired of hearing the story about his mishap told over and over, but his friend kept exaggerating about how high and how long he was suspended in the air. It also reminded him of how sore his body still was.

"The kids said they saw a strange-looking bird in the air," Mrs. Robert said. "I believe them."

"Where did you see it?" Ranger Bill said, rising to his feet.

"I only saw its shadow," Justin said. "It was down

15

by Alger Island, just after we passed the lighthouse and headed back for camp."

"Then that is where we'll begin our search," Ranger Bill said. "Thank you so much for the lemonade." Handing his empty glass to Mrs. Robert, he turned to the Adirondack kids. "I had a hunch stopping here would be helpful. Thank you all for the valuable information."

"Wow, Jackie," Justin said. "A pelican? That would be a great bird to add to your 'life list'."

Nick agreed. "Yes," he said. "It's too bad you were so busy bent over in the boat trying to grab Dax, or you would have seen it too."

Jackie shook her head. "Brown Pelicans live way down south," she said. "What is it doing way up here in the Adirondacks?"

Justin shrugged. "We saw a loon one time when we were on our winter vacation in Myrtle Beach, right, Mom?" he said.

Mrs. Robert smiled. "Yes, we did."

"Where's Myrtle Beach?" Nick asked.

"South Carolina," Jackie said.

"Where's South Carolina?" Nick asked.

"Are you kidding?" Jackie said. "You don't know where South Carolina is? It is where your grandparents live."

Nick shrugged. "Sure I know where South Carolina is," he said and guessed. "Somewhere near North Carolina?" He grinned.

"Show them the loon, Mom," Justin said.

"I'd love to," Mrs. Robert said. "Come in for a moment, I'll show you a photograph."

Everyone pushed through the front screen door to gather around the computer near the fireplace in the camp's living room. Mrs. Robert hit a few keys, and there on the monitor appeared a photograph of a common loon resting on an open, ocean beach.

"It sure is strange seeing a loon just sitting there in the sand like that," Jackie said. "And with all those beach houses so near."

"I never saw a loon when I was down south," Nick said.

"This loon was ill," Mrs. Robert said. "We contacted the U.S. Fish and Wildlife office, and waited until someone with a proper license came to rescue it."

"We were the only ones who even knew what kind of a bird it was," Justin said. "Everyone who was walking on the beach stopped to see it and asked us if it was laying eggs!"

"Well, a common loon in South Carolina is not so unusual," Ranger Bill said. "When the lakes ice up around here, our Adirondack loons fly out and do spend their winters out on the ocean. But this pelican, so far north and all alone?" He adjusted his cap and let out a deep breath. "It doesn't belong here at all."

"But it can't be hurt," Nick said. "When it was following Justin, it was flying really good."

Ranger Bill swung the screen door open to leave. "Just because a bird looks healthy, it doesn't necessarily mean it is," he said. "We're not yet sure how

17

Mrs. Robert hit a few keys.
There on the monitor appeared a photograph
of a common loon on an ocean beach.

18

this pelican got so far off course, but of one thing we are very sure – if we don't find and capture that bird soon, it won't survive."

Chapter Five

The Labor Day Bear Strikes Again?

Nick snapped the end off a long stick to make a pointy end and poked a marshmallow on it.

Justin frowned. "How many marshmallows are you going to cook at once?" he said. "You've got three going now – it's not fair."

The small campfire near the lean-to crackled underneath the roasting marshmallows that were quickly turning brown in the flickering flames.

"It's not my fault I can do a bunch of things at the same time," Nick said.

"Don't worry, Justin," Jackie said. "I brought extra." She waved a large, plastic bag stuffed with puffy white treats for all to see.

Nick grinned.

"Plus," Jackie continued. "I am in charge of all the chocolate bars and graham crackers." She likewise displayed those packages of treats to the boys, who were a safe distance across from her. "Nobody makes another s'more without coming to me."

Nick stopped grinning.

The shadows of nightfall were slowly stealing

across the cloud-streaked northern sky. As darkness pressed in, beams from a full moon reflecting off the lake promised some welcome extra light.

"Do you think the Labor Day Bear is going to ruin our sleepover again this year?" Justin asked. The question lingered in the air with the smoke above the fire.

Nick popped a toasted marshmallow into his mouth. "I hope not," he said, more concerned with assembling his next sticky sweet than with worry over what he considered a phantom bear.

Jackie carefully placed no more than two graham cracker squares and one chocolate bar into the outstretched hand of an unhappy Nick. "No one has reported seeing the bear yet," she said. "Not even the Pie Lady."

The Pie Lady. She seemed to be the annual victim of the Labor Day Bear, as she simply refused to refrain from setting her pies outside on her porch railing to cool in the chill of the early morning air. She baked every weekend all summer and was determined that no creature, no matter how large or small, was going to change her routine. And for the last three years, the Labor Day Bear seemed to get at least one of her pies. The battle had become so famous along the north shore of the lake, the Adirondack kids had even made a game out of it.

"I wonder why the bear only shows up on Labor Day weekend," Justin said.

"Maybe it's his vacation," Nick said, and laughed

21

out loud – alone.

"What I think is amazing is that someone always sends the Pie Lady a note with some money in it to replace whatever she loses," Jackie said. "Some people are so nice."

"Could you be one of those nice people and pass me some more marshmallows?" Nick said.

Jackie was careless this time. Nick lunged forward and grabbed the entire bag before she could stop him.

"Well, if that bear dares to show up here, we'll just make a lot of noise like we did to chase that big one away that attacked our tent in the high peaks," Justin said.*

Dax suddenly emerged from the creeping darkness and startled them all. She sniffed the ground at their feet in search of crumbs from a sloppy cook.

"Let's talk about something else," Nick said, as he shoved three more marshmallows onto a single stick and thrust the stack into the fire. "Like about the pelican."

"What about the pelican?" Justin asked.

Nick momentarily stared into the fire, as if mesmerized by the flames. "Well," he said. "Do you think Ranger Bill is right? Could the pelican really be in a lot of trouble if someone doesn't find it?"

Before anyone could answer, Nick's three marshmallows suddenly burst into flames.

The explosion caused Justin to fall off his seat and drop his stick in the dirt. He yelled as he scrambled to his feet. "That bird isn't in as much trouble as you

22

are," he said. "Stop wasting all the marshmallows."

Nick stood to face him. "I didn't do it on purpose," he shot back. "You don't want to waste any?" He pointed the stick with the marshmallows' pitiful charred remains toward Justin. "Have one!"

"Will you two stop it," Jackie said. "Or, I'm joining Dax."

Justin bent over to pick up his stick and looked around. "Where did she go?" he said. "Here Daxy. Here girl."

"I don't know where she went," Jackie said. "She just took off. And I am leaving, too, if you both won't just sit down and be quiet."

A low growl from somewhere behind the lean-to caused them all to freeze. They stared at one another with eyes wide open, daring only to move their eyelids as they blinked.

* see *The Adirondack Kids® #5, Islands in the Sky*

Chapter Six

A Change in Plans

Not one of the Adirondack kids could remember their sneakers even touching the ground the night before as they raced to Justin's camp for safety.

"Who put the campfire out?" Jackie asked, as the three friends dared to take a morning walk around the lean-to. They examined the area surrounding the small pit of black ash that was now littered with the burned and broken sticks that had been their cooking utensils.

Justin sighed. "My dad came down and put it out for us," he said.

"And the bear took all the marshmallows and the crackers and the chocolate?" Nick said. He kept walking in circles around the lean-to. "All of it is gone?"

Justin nodded. "Everything," he said.

"We were stupid," Jackie said. "We should have known better than to be out cooking all that food. We knew there was a good chance the bear could be around this weekend."

Nick shrugged and defended their decision. "We didn't know for sure he would even be back again this year," he said. Then he kicked the logs they had used as seats and foot stools, hoping as they rolled over he might find at least one surviving candy bar. "Are you sure your dad didn't eat the rest?"

Justin shook his head. "Positive," he said, and paused. "So, that's it then. No laker, no more s'mores and no Labor Day sleepover."

There was an awkward silence.

"I have an idea," Jackie said. "Follow me." She ran to the dock and jumped into her small aluminum boat, the one they called the putt-putt. It rocked in the water as she scrambled to position herself at the engine.

Justin and Nick ran to join her.

"Where are you going?" Justin said.

"Let's go to the island for some breakfast," Jackie said. "You two haven't been to our place for almost the whole summer." She pulled the cord to start the engine and it erupted to life. "Maybe my mom and dad will let us have a sleepover on the lawn this weekend." She smiled. "We could still see the fireworks from there, and there won't be any bears, unless they want to take a long swim."

"Well, maybe," Justin said.

"That's a maybe, and a maybe is yes," Jackie said. "Come on, let's go."

Justin was glad to have a friend like Jackie. She always seemed to find a way to turn a disappointing situation into something good. The island her camp was on was small, with very little yard space, and so there was no lean-to. But it would be space on the lake, under the stars, and safe! And with a perfect view of the fireworks. "Okay," he said, smiling for the first time that morning.

As he called out to his mom for permission to head for the island, Dax appeared and pranced over to the side of the boat. The calico stood there as if waiting for a formal invitation.

"Yes, you can come, too, girl," Justin said. He scooped her up and together they settled into the front seat.

"Jump in, Nick," Jackie said. "You sit in the middle."

"I can't come with you," Nick said.

"Why not?" Justin said. "We'll drive over to your dock and you can ask your mom too."

Nick stood staring out at the lake. "It's the pelican," he said.

Jackie laughed. "You're not getting me to turn around and look," she said. "Just get into the boat."

"I'm being honest," Nick said. "There isn't time to take me to my camp." He pointed. "I mean it. The pelican is going to get away."

Jackie and Justin turned to see the southern bird gliding through the northern air across the middle of the lake in the general direction of Inlet.

"There it is!" Justin said. "It's flying really fast."

Without hesitation, Jackie masterfully maneuvered the boat away from the dock and out into the open water.

As the putt-putt charged through the waves, Nick

ran up the hill and along the shoreline to urge them on. "Go!" he said. "Go! Go! Go!"

Jackie laughed. "You're not going to get me
to turn around and look," she said.

Chapter Seven

The Pie Lady

As the hum of the putt-putt grew fainter, Nick stopped running and realized he had already traveled along the shoreline past his own camp and was almost halfway to the home of the Pie Lady.

He had reached the section of the path where it narrowed and was becoming overgrown with tall grass. Nick wasn't much of a risk taker, but he didn't like the fact that his friends were off having an adventure without him.

Curiosity about whether or not the Pie Lady's pies had been eaten again by the Labor Day Bear overcame his fear that the creature might be waiting to pounce from some hiding place in the tall grass along the path. Taking a deep breath, he decided to move forward, reasoning it would be much more likely the bear was off somewhere asleep on its back, snoring with a belly full of s'mores. *I hope he has a stomach ache for a month*, he thought.

The second half of the hike along the path seemed to take forever. He had just made out what appeared to be the end of the trail, which helped relax some of the tightness he felt in his stomach, when something to his left in the tall grass moved.

Something that was really big.

Instinct took over and he darted sideways toward the lake away from the movement, and yelled. In a flash he imagined himself diving into the water and swimming for his life!

How relieved he was to see the white tail of an equally frightened deer disappearing into some crowded pines.

The lone Adirondack kid, who indeed felt very lonely now, trotted ahead until the path emptied into a well manicured yard that was wide and green and sloped downward onto a private sandy beach. And there at the top of the hill sat a large square building with chocolate-brown shingles and white trim, which was the home of the Pie Lady.

Nick walked down to the beach and looked out on the lake to see if he could spot his friends. There were a lot of boats, but no sign of the putt-putt or the pelican.

He looked down at the easy waves, the water lapping around his sneakers that were pressed into the dark, wet sand. Scanning the entire patch of private beach, he saw no footprints of man or beast, other than his own.

The tinkling of wind chimes drew his attention back up to the house. The sound lured him up the lawn to a side porch that featured a long and unusually wide, flat railing. A wide, flat railing that was lined with pies.

The chimes chattered again in the slight breeze that suddenly shifted in Nick's direction and carried a sweet bouquet of aromas to his nostrils. He closed his eyes, breathed in deeply and, as if in a trance, slowly began to ascend the stairs.

Blackberry, raspberry, strawberry, he thought. *Oh, there's a pumpkin and an apple – yes – that's definitely an apple.*

His heavenly moment ended abruptly as a short elderly woman wearing a checkered apron and wielding a long-handled broom burst through the porch door and charged straight at him. "Two pies weren't enough?" she said. Her voice boomed from a face that was wrinkled and stern. "I knew I'd finally catch you!"

Chapter Eight

Chasing the Cruiser

With Dax perched in her favorite position on the bow of the boat and Justin seated right behind her, Jackie tried to keep the putt-putt up to speed with the pelican as it cut through the air, gliding back and forth over the water between the hamlets of Inlet and Eagle Bay. Whenever the bird came near one of the many holiday vessels dotting the lake, it would soar downward and fly closely by, startling a few of the boaters, and thrilling all of them.

For a few minutes the bird even flew over the putt-putt, giving Justin a close-up look at the winged creature that had spoiled his laker. It was a pelican all right. Like Nick, he remembered well seeing plenty of the prehistoric-looking creatures while on family vacation, but usually there were at least three of the birds flying together in loose formation, skimming the ocean surf.

Jackie called out over the hum of the putt-putt's engine. "It looks like it's searching for something," she said.

Justin nodded in agreement.

The two Adirondack kids watched as one poor soul stood up in a canoe in an attempt to take a picture of the goose-sized bird as it flew by. They could see the other passenger in the canoe gripping the gunwales as the unstable vessel began rocking, and they knew what was coming.

Sure enough, within seconds it was man and camera overboard. Zooming by in the putt-putt, Justin and Jackie could tell the dry passenger wasn't happy at all as she helped her soaking companion scramble back into the canoe.

By now the rare bird had attracted quite a bit of attention, as people everywhere out on the lake were pointing skyward with fingers and paddles and fishing poles.

Justin turned to look at Jackie. "Don't pelicans ever get tired?" he said. "If it doesn't land soon, we're going to run out of gas."

Jackie shrugged. "It's got to stop flying sometime," she said. "But if we see it land on one of the islands or somewhere on the main shore, we have to go back and call Ranger Bill right away." She pointed ahead. "Look, it's headed for Cedar Island right now."

Justin nodded. "Good," he said. "Maybe it will take some time to rest."

The bird was indeed getting ready to land, but not on the island. Intercepting the cruise boat passing in front of the island, the pelican gathered its wings and came to rest on the roof in front of the smokestack, which was just above the captain at the wheel.

"Oh, great," Justin said. "Now the pelican could end up all the way back to Old Forge Pond!"

The bow of the putt-putt lifted Dax high into the air as Jackie picked up speed to see if she could get alongside the cruiser. Justin pulled his bucket hat snugly onto his head so it wouldn't blow away.

"Maybe we can get the captain to notice the bird and he can get a radio message to Ranger Bill," Jackie said. She kept the putt-putt a safe distance away while gradually overtaking the massive boat.

As Jackie and Justin waved and pointed toward the feathered stowaway in an effort to get the captain's attention, friendly tourists on the upper and lower decks pointed and waved back. Some even began taking photographs of them.

"This isn't working," Justin said.

"I don't know what else we can do," Jackie said.

"Maybe it will help if you can get us a little closer," Justin said.

"No way," Jackie said. "That would be too dangerous."

The cruise boat was nearing the end of the bay and was headed swiftly back down the Fulton Chain.

Justin protested. "Come on, Jackie, we have to do something," he said.

The debate ended abruptly with the bellowing sound of the cruise boat's horn. It was the horn that sat on the roof in front of the smokestack and above the captain. It was the horn right next to the pelican.

The bow of the putt-putt lifted Dax
into the air as Jackie picked up speed...

"Wait, there it goes," Justin said. They watched as the bird launched into the sky and turned back toward the bay. "We have to go back. It's headed for Cedar Island again."

Jackie slowed down allowing the cruise boat to speed on by them. Using the tiller, she caused the putt-putt to move in a small arc, cutting through the vessel's wake. "I think we can still catch up before it gets away," she said.

And that was when the putt-putt, with engine still roaring, stopped dead in the water.

Chapter Nine

Going Nowhere Fast

A bewildered Justin looked back at his bewildered captain. "What's wrong?" he said.

Jackie twisted the throttle on the tiller causing the engine to race, but the putt-putt remained in place, only rising and falling on the final waves created by the passing cruise boat. She grunted in frustration. "I don't know what's wrong," she said, and turned off the engine.

"Did we run out of gas?" Justin said, trying to be helpful.

"How could we be out of gas?" Jackie said. "Didn't you just hear the engine running?"

They watched as the pelican became smaller and smaller and then somewhere near Cedar Island seemed to drop out of sight.

Jackie turned to gain some leverage and tipped the motor's power head toward her, which lifted the rest of the engine out of the water. She shook her head. "It's gone."

"I know," Justin said, still watching for any sign of the pelican. "But I think it landed somewhere on the island."

"Not the pelican," Jackie said. "The propeller."

Justin peered over her shoulder. Water was still dripping from the long metal shaft that had been raised out of the lake. "What happened to it?" he said. "Did we hit something?" He looked all around for any buoys marking shallow waters. There weren't any. "I don't get it. We didn't bump against a rock or anything."

Jackie shrugged and eased the engine back into place. "Somehow it just fell off," she said. "I guess we're going to row."

Justin looked at the heavy wooden oars that would have to be lifted and placed into the oar locks. His arms suddenly felt heavy and he hadn't even touched one yet. While thankful for a way to move the boat forward, he couldn't think of a task he dreaded more. He looked up at the sun. Although high in the sky, he still wondered if they would have enough remaining daylight to paddle all the way back to camp.

Dax began to curl up on a small bed of life jackets as if she knew to settle in for a long ride, when a familiar horn sounded from a fast-approaching boat that was headed in their direction.

"It's Captain McBride!" Justin said, thrilled that he and Jackie wouldn't have to wrestle with the oars.

Captain Conall McBride waved from the helm of his mail boat, *Miss America*, as he coasted in and idled alongside the helpless putt-putt. "Run out of gas again, my dear friends?" he said.*

38

"Not this time," Justin said.

"Somehow we lost our propeller," Jackie said.

A second voice called down from the deck of the mail boat. "Here, attach the tow rope to your bow."

"Ranger Bill!" Justin said.

Neither Justin nor Jackie recognized yet another passenger who was already lowering a rope ladder to aid them in boarding the mail boat.

Ranger Bill called out some friendly orders. "Let's get going," he said and smiled. "We have a pelican to rescue."

---

* see *The Adirondack Kids® #3 – The Lost Lighthouse*

Chapter Ten

Meet Sydney Hunter

As the *Miss America* plowed through the Fourth Lake waters toward Cedar Island with the putt-putt in tow, Justin and Jackie waited with the captain who was steering from his cabin while Ranger Bill and the stranger stood at the bow of the boat talking and peering through their binoculars.

"She's not wearing a green uniform, so she's not a ranger," Justin said. "What kind of police person wears a brown and tan uniform?"

"Did you see the patch on her shoulder?" Jackie said. "It said something about fish on it."

Justin had not noticed the words on the patch, but he did see something of the design. "I thought I saw a bird on it," he said. "Maybe it was a pelican."

"Ah-choo!" Dax had not been on board for more than five minutes, and the color of Captain McBride's nose was already turning rosy red. "I have missed Dax this summer," he said. "But I have not missed sneezing!"

Justin was holding his adopted calico and stroking her head behind her ears, making her eyes squint. "I still can't believe you let me have her," he said. "I can't imagine ever being without her now."

Everyone who ever heard the captain's jolly laugh could not help but smile. Somehow he even made sad news sound happy. "And I couldn't imagine sneezing all summer long," he said. "Obviously the allergy I have to my former assistant is never going away, so giving her up for adoption to you was the right thing to do." He slowed the mail boat down as they approached the edge of the island. "Dax took a great liking to you and I was thrilled she could find such a wonderful owner and home." He sneezed and pointed toward the bow of the boat. "Ranger Bill is motioning for you to join him. It appears all of you are here for the same reason." He winked and sneezed again.

As the *Miss America* slowed to a near stop, Ranger Bill introduced the stranger.

"Justin and Jackie, I'd like you to meet Sydney Hunter," he said. "Ms. Hunter is with the U.S. Fish & Wildlife Service."

"Please call me Sydney," she said.

"It's a duck," Justin said, as he shook her outstretched hand.

Sydney looked at the cat he was holding and laughed. "Pardon me?" she said.

Jackie reached out to shake her hand and apologized for her tactless friend. "Not the cat," she said. "That's Dax." She pointed to her shoulder. "He means the duck on your patch."

"We were just trying to figure out who you are," Justin said. "I thought if you had a pelican on your patch, you might be someone who helps pelicans."

"Well, I do help with pelicans and all kinds of wildlife," Sydney said. She pointed to the bird resting on a large boulder on the island shore. "And today I am here to help with this wayward pelican."

While they watched, the bird took off again, landing this time on the bow of a boat not much bigger than the putt-putt. Two startled fishermen huddled at the stern of their vessel.

"This pelican is famished," Sydney said.

"But it looks perfectly fine," Jackie said.

Justin agreed. "We even saw it up close. How can you tell it's hungry?"

Sydney raised her binoculars. "Many people don't understand that starving birds can still appear quite healthy and not look bad at all, until just before they die."

"That's right," Ranger Bill said. "This bird's behavior—the way it is acting—is showing us it is in trouble."

Justin did not like hearing this at all. Neither did Jackie.

"But we have to do something," Justin said. "Don't we?"

Sydney lowered her binoculars, looked at Justin and smiled. "I can't make any promises that we will be able to save this pelican," she said. "But Ranger Bill and I have worked out a plan, and we are sure going to try." Justin could not believe what he heard

42

her say next. "And we would like both you and Jackie to help."

Justin recovered quickly from the shock. "And Nick," he said.

"Nick?" Sydney said. "Who is Nick?"

Chapter Eleven

2 Kayaks, Some Fish and a Sheet

"Hunter?" Nick said. "She's a hunter?" He looked over at the woman in the tan uniform standing on the dock with Ranger Bill and Justin's parents. She was the youngest and tallest adult among them and had dark hair that was pulled into a pony tail, like Jackie's. "She sure looks nice enough." He turned back to his friends. "So why is she going to shoot the pelican? We're not going to let her, right?"

Justin laughed. "She's not a hunter," he said. "Her first name is Sydney and her last name is Hunter."

Jackie poked him. "She just introduced herself to you," she said. "Sydney Hunter. Don't you ever listen?"

Nick raised both of his hands. "I need you guys to listen to me," he said.

"We don't have time," Justin said. "If we're going to save the pelican, we have to try right now."

Nick persisted. "But it's about the Pie Lady."

"Are you three all set to go?" It was Ranger Bill. "Nick, we've already called the restaurant and they are expecting you."

"We really need those fish," Jackie said. "It's a main part of the plan."

Nick moaned. "I don't want to ride my bike all the way back into town," he said. Then his eyes brightened. "Hey, let's use the fish I caught here while I was waiting for you guys to get back." He ran over to the large white pail at the edge of the dock. Peering into it, he frowned.

"I think they want you to go to the restaurant to get the kind of fish the pelican is used to eating at the ocean," Jackie said.

"It doesn't matter," Nick said. "Someone dumped all the ones I caught back into the lake. I was going to let the pelican eat Stegosaurus. I'm so sick of that old rock bass sticking me with the spines on his back every single time I catch him."* He cupped his hands around his mouth and yelled down at the water. "You got lucky again this time, Stego!" he said.

"Nick, we need you to go right now!" Ranger Bill said.

Nick addressed Justin and Jackie as he ran by them to get his bike. "If the pelican ate Stego, it would probably make the poor bird even sicker anyway," he said. Then he was up the hill and gone.

Mr. and Mrs. Robert were pulling two kayaks out of the boathouse, while Justin and Jackie plucked two life jackets from the helpless putt-putt that was tied to the dock.

"I can't believe you're letting me go," Justin said to his parents, as they eased the two boats into the

45

water alongside the dock. "I thought you weren't going to let me take the kayak again until next summer." **

"Well, your mom and I talked about it and both of us felt you have grown up quite a bit during the past two months," Mr. Robert said.

"We can trust you to make good choices now – yes?" Mrs. Robert said.

Justin beamed. "Yes, you can," he said.

His mom smiled. "And we will all be right here watching to make sure you do," she said, and winked.

Ranger Bill and Sydney gave the two paddlers some final instructions.

"The way your family's dock is built, it sweeps around and acts like a fence creating a nice little corral here," Ranger Bill said. "So if the pelican lands in the water, work together to herd the bird this way and try to drive it between the dock and shoreline."

Justin shook his head. "I get it," he said. "Kind of like what cowboys do when they round up cattle."

"And cowgirls," Jackie reminded him.

Sydney laughed. "We'll be hidden and when the bird gets close enough, we'll throw a sheet over it to capture it and keep it calm and safe," she said.

"What if we scare the pelican before it gets in the trap?" Justin said.

"When the pelican lands in the water, don't get too excited," Ranger Bill said. "This bird obviously isn't afraid of boats, so just take your time. Don't be in a rush."

Mr. and Mrs. Robert held the kayaks in place on the water at the edge of the dock while Justin and Jackie climbed into them. Ranger Bill and Sydney handed them each their paddles.

Justin zipped up his life jacket. With all the fuss over the two of them, he felt for a moment like he and Jackie were being prepared for a special mission, like in an action movie. Then he realized that's exactly what was happening. They were on a special mission, but with no guarantee for success.

"I've got one more question before we go," Justin said. "What if the pelican doesn't land in the water at all? What if it just flies away or lands on another boat and disappears, like it almost did on the cruise boat?"

Sydney nodded. "That certainly could happen," she said.

Mr. Robert knelt down beside him. "We go to church every Sunday, right, Son?" he said. Justin nodded. "You know what to do then." Offering his parting advice, he gave Justin's kayak a gentle push away from the dock. "Pray!"

* see *The Adirondack Kids® #7 - Mystery of the Missing Moose*

**see *The Adirondack Kids® #1*

Chapter Twelve

An Unidentified Floating Object

"Don't get so far ahead of me," Justin said. He liked the red kayak because it was smaller and felt easier to paddle. But it did not track as well in the water as the larger one, making it more difficult for him to stay on course and keep up with his friend.

Jackie was in the larger green kayak and slowed down until he caught up with her. "Sorry, Justin," she said.

Together they paddled toward the area they had last seen the bird. The warm glow of late afternoon light seemed to be a signal for boaters to head for their camps to get ready for supper.

Jackie noticed the quiet on the water. "There are a lot less boats for the pelican to visit now," she said.

"But where did it go?" Justin said. "We haven't seen it flying around out here since Captain McBride dropped us off." He plunged his paddle into the water and held it there, causing his kayak to spin sideways. "I'm checking to see if it's sneaking up behind us."

Jackie joined him and with a few more easy strokes they were fully facing the shore. They both noticed a small shape moving out on the Robert's dock.

"Is that Nick already?" Justin said. "Why is he running around out in the open? He should be hiding."

"Maybe he's setting up the bait," Jackie said. Justin didn't answer. "You know," she said, "the fish from the restaurant." Still no reply. She looked over at him. "Justin?"

"Is that a loon?" Justin said. He pointed with his paddle at a spot directly between them and the camp.

"I can't tell," Jackie said. "I know there are no buoys anywhere near there." She motioned toward one of the last speedboats on the lake that was about to cut between them and the unidentified floating object. "We should know what it is in a second."

As the boat sliced through the water and approached the object, a winged creature lifted into the air and as the boat passed by, it dropped back down with a small splash. It was the only hint they needed.

"It's the pelican!" Justin said. "Let's go!" His paddle banged against Jackie's kayak next to him.

"Justin!" she said. "What did Ranger Bill say?"

The waves of the speed boat passed underneath them. "I know," he said, and took a deep breath. "He said not to hurry."

"Good," Jackie said. Then with a calmness that matched the growing stillness of the water she said, "Now we'll go."

The closer Justin and Jackie got to the stationary

bird, the more they moved their boats apart, the red kayak to the left and the green kayak to the right.

Justin began to chant. "Please don't fly away. Please don't fly away. Please don't fly away."

"Shhhh!" Jackie said, trying to use her inner voice. "Keep that up and it *will* fly away. I can hear you way over here."

Dipping their paddles into the water sparingly and very gently, they managed to coast close enough to the bird that they could now see details in its head and neck and body, including its eye, which in the center was the blue of the late summer sky and ringed with sunset pink.

The two naval members of the rescue team stopped paddling.

Justin whispered. "Why isn't it moving?" he said.

Jackie whispered back. "Maybe Sydney is right. Maybe it's a lot weaker than we thought."

Two people and a bird sat motionless, three points forming a small scalene triangle in the middle of the lake.

Justin accidentally bumped his paddle against his kayak and grimaced, fearing the sound would cause the bird to explode suddenly into the air. But then he smiled, as instead the dull thud seemed to encourage the pelican to swim forward.

Together the unlikely trio moved steadily toward the shore. If the pelican would swim too far left, Justin would paddle his red kayak further left and drive it back to the right. When the bird would drift too far to the right, Jackie would paddle her green kayak further right and coax it back to the left.

Approaching the dock, the paddlers eased the pelican in the direction of the man-made corral.

Justin caught a glimpse of his parents kneeling down, hiding in the bushes along the shore. Ranger Bill and Sydney were in the shadows, crouching just inside the open mouth of the boathouse. He tried not to laugh out loud seeing what looked like a bunch of grownups playing a game of hide-and-seek. *They're not very good at it,* he thought. He noticed Jackie's broad smile and knew she saw them too.

"Where's Nick?" Justin whispered across to his partner.

Jackie scanned the landscape. "I see him," she whispered back. "Look up on the hill. Near the camp. By the trail." She paused. "I think he's holding Dax."

Justin looked up to catch a glimpse of his friend when his smiling face suddenly transformed into one twisted by fear. And that was when the quiet was broken with a desperate cry. "Look out, Nick!" Justin shouted. "Bear!"

Chapter Thirteen

Bird on Board

Justin's sudden and piercing outburst caused the bear to bolt away and the pelican to skip across the water and lift off into the air right in front of the Robert's dock. "Oh, no," he said.

Satisfied Nick and Dax were out of danger, he turned awkwardly in his kayak and craned his neck upward in an attempt to relocate the pelican. He had seen the bird turn gracefully away from the tall evergreens above their camp and it appeared to be gliding back toward the wide-open sky over the lake. All the shifting and twisting in his kayak to try and locate the bird was making him dizzy.

"Look out, Justin." It was Jackie, who was positioned behind her bewildered friend and could easily follow the pelican's flight pattern. "It's coming back around."

"Where is it?" Justin asked as his kayak continued to coast toward the cove. "I can't see it." As he righted himself in the seat of his rocking craft, the answer dropped out of the sky and with a loud thump landed firmly on his bow.

The pelican dropped out of the sky and
with a loud thump, landed on Justin's boat.

"Now!" shouted someone from the shore, and within seconds a large billowing sheet was floating high over boat and bird and boy.

Sailing blind with the sheet draped over him, Justin could hear the sound of excited voices and feet pounding on the dock. There was even some splashing in the water right next to him.

"I've got the bird," he heard someone say.

"Be careful, that beak can be dangerous," someone else said.

He felt a slight bump and he knew the kayak had finally come to rest against the dock.

There was applause and he heard Jackie say, "You did it, Justin." Then the sheet was pulled off from him, taking with it his bucket hat. Before he could protest he helplessly watched as Sydney, with the pelican wrapped and calm and firmly in her grasp, hustled up the hill. A vehicle with its motor running was waiting for her in front of the camp.

"Who is that in the car?" Justin asked, as his dad helped him out of the kayak. "Where is Sydney going? Is the pelican going to be all right?"

Ranger Bill laughed. "Sydney isn't going anywhere," he said. "She is giving the pelican to Emily, who is a licensed rehabilitator."

"Emily is going to drive the pelican to a Wild Bird Clinic in Delaware where they can most effectively help birds that are injured or sick," Mrs. Robert said. "And they specialize in pelicans."

"Where is Delaware?" Nick asked.

54

Jackie shook her head. "Where's Myrtle Beach? Where's South Carolina? Where's Delaware?" she said, mimicking the sound of Nick's voice. "I'm just going to get you a poster of the United States for your bedroom."

"As soon as I get a solid word on the condition of our pelican, I will let all of you know," Ranger Bill said. He looked at Justin and Jackie. "Congratulations to both of you. Without your help, this bird would not likely have had a chance."

"What about me?" Nick said, ready for some special recognition and praise.

"We'll give you credit for keeping Dax safe," Justin said. He looked around. "Where did you put her?"

Nick shrugged. "I don't know," he said. "She jumped out of my arms and took off down the trail."

Justin was stunned. "You mean she took off after the bear?" he said.

"What bear?" Nick asked.

Justin was already running.

Chapter Fourteen

Strung Along

"I know we can catch up to Dax before she catches up to the bear," Justin said. He belted out instructions between gasps for air as he ran. "Help me call out her name. I know that will keep the bear moving away. And it might bring Dax back to us."

"Justin, wait!" Jackie called.

After so many years of friendship, Justin recognized it wasn't only the words, but the way she said the words that made a difference. There was urgency in Jackie's voice. As anxious as he was to find Dax, he knew he had to stop. "What is it?" he said, panting more from worry than from sprinting.

"You stepped right into a pie tin," Jackie said. She could tell Justin could not believe she had stopped him to tell him that, so she held the pie tin up.

Justin looked down at his sneakers. "It wasn't me," he said. "And Nick still hasn't even caught up to us."

"Well, somebody stepped into it," Jackie said. "Have you ever seen a bear leave a pie tin half full? Why isn't the pie tin licked clean? Doesn't that seem a little bit strange to you?"

"Hey, come here you guys." It was Nick. "I found the ball of string from the kite I lost last week," he said. "The wind was so strong it yanked everything right out of my hands. I wondered where it landed. Come and help me find my kite."

"I can't believe you even tried to fly a kite around here with trees everywhere," Jackie said.

Nick shrugged. "It's the end of summer," he said. "It was on sale. There were lots of them left."

Jackie pointed to the giant conifer trees that lined the shore. "I wonder why?" she said.

Justin was not happy. "Are you two going to stand here all day and play detective and scavenger hunt, or are you going to help me find Dax?"

"Hey, come and look at my string," Nick said. "It's moving!"

It was true. They gathered to see the ball of string that was stuck on a branch in a bush was unreeling from the kite handle at an astonishing rate.

Nick whistled. "It's moving faster than a fishing line with a muskie on the end of it," he said.

"Maybe the end of it got caught on Dax," Justin said.

"Or the bear," Nick said.

Jackie shook her head. "Something about all this just isn't right," she said.

Still attached to the kite handle that was caught in the branches, the string suddenly ran out and became taut causing the bush to shake. Before any of them could grab it, the handle broke free, bouncing and snaking off down the trail.

"Don't let it get away," Justin said. "It might lead us to Dax."

The three Adirondack kids chased their only clue down the trail and all the way into the open lawn at the Pie Lady's house.

Nick was panting. "I've got to stop a minute," he said. "I've got to rest."

Justin and Jackie didn't wait. They ran across the lawn and up the driveway still chasing the kite handle into a small field located between the chocolate-brown house and the Forest Inn.

"You again!" boomed a familiar voice accompanied by the bang of a door slamming open and the sound of pounding footsteps moving rapidly across the porch floor. "Three pies weren't enough?"

Three pies? Nick thought. He didn't even turn to look. Bolting after his friends, he could still imagine the baker's stern face and long-handled broom coming straight at him.

Chapter Fifteen

In the Forest Inn

"It's gone," Justin said. "I have no idea which way the string went. This grass is too tall." He knelt down and picked up a broken stick with some brown colored paper on it.

"Hey, that's a piece of my kite," Nick said, finally catching up to his friends.

Jackie moved slowly through the grass and found a larger piece. "It couldn't have been shaped like a rectangle," she said. "This looks like part of a wing?" She held it up. "What kind of a kite was it?"

"It was an eagle," Nick said. "That was why I bought that one. You know, for Eagle Bay?" He grinned.

Justin moved forward. The kite's skeletal remains seemed to litter the field. "All these pieces are leading to the Forest Inn," he said.

"Hey, there's the eagle's head," Nick said. "Over there in the parking lot. Let's go get it."

The Forest Inn was one of the grandest buildings in Inlet, positioned perfectly for dining while overlooking the sun as it set on the lake. A number of people in fancy clothes walked past them and up the stairs to the front door.

"Should we go in?" Justin said.

"I don't think we're dressed right," Nick said.

Jackie sighed. "You want to find Dax, right?"

Justin shook his head. "Yes," he said.

"Okay, then," Jackie said and began marching up the stairs. "Let's find out if anyone has seen her."

A woman with a wide smile greeted them just inside the door. She reached for several menus. "Dinner for five?" she said.

Nick looked around. "There are only three of us," hc said. He whispered to Jackie. "I might not know where Dclaware is, but I can count."

"Oh," the woman said. "I thought you might be with your parents."

"No, Ma'am," Justin said. "We were just wondering if you saw a cat come in here a little while ago?"

"Or a bear," Nick said.

"A cat?" the woman said. "A bear?"

"A calico cat," Justin said. "You couldn't miss her. She is black and rufous on top and white underneath and her back left leg has stripes like on a tiger."

"And she has a large black triangle on her face," Jackie said. "Everybody notices that about her."

"Well, no, I'm sorry," the woman said. "I have not seen a single cat today." She looked at Nick. "Nor have I seen a bear."

"Are you sure you haven't seen my cat?" Justin said. "She is pretty sneaky. Maybe someone else who works here has seen her."

The woman cleared her throat. "Well, you children will have to excuse me now," she said. "There is a line beginning to form behind you."

"I have to use the bathroom," Nick said.

"Pardon me?" the woman said. She looked toward the front door that was propped open now with people starting to gather out on the stairs.

Nick began to beg. "Please, can I use the bathroom?" he said.

"No, well, yes," the woman said, working hard to maintain her smile. "Yes, go ahead." She motioned to the left with the menus still in her hand. "It is right down those stairs."

Justin could tell the woman didn't really want to let Nick use the bathroom, but she seemed desperate to serve the waiting customers. As they trotted down the stairs, he urged his friend to hurry. "We need to get back outside and find Dax," he said. "I want to find her before it gets dark."

"Dax is probably already back at camp," Jackie said. "She is one of the smartest cats I've ever known. Sometimes you worry too much."

"I'm not taking any chances," Justin said. He knew Jackie was right – that maybe he did overreact at times. But after an entire summer of adventures with Dax, he simply could not imagine a day without her.

"I only sort of need to use the bathroom," Nick said.

"What do you mean?" Jackie said.

"I saw this on the floor at the top of the stairs," Nick said. He opened his palm which cradled a small piece of yellow paper.

"What is that?" Justin said.

"Part of my eagle's beak," Nick said.

"So, whatever was dragging your kite has got to be in here somewhere," Jackie said.

Justin agreed. "Then that means," he said, "it couldn't have been a bear."

Chapter Sixteen

Dax Cracks the Case

"Where is that music coming from?" Justin said.

"I don't know," Nick said. "But it sounds really bad – like music for old people."

"This way," Jackie said.

A hallway led from the bathrooms to another small dining area. Several large paintings of Adirondack landscapes adorned the walls and two over-sized picture windows offered a commanding view of the lake. The room appeared empty, except for some tables dressed in white tablecloths and a guitar player sitting on a stool in a corner.

"I told you," Nick said. "That's where you get put when you are really bad – in the corner."

"Hello there," the guitar player said. "I'm just practicing, getting ready for the evening crowd. Come on in and join us." He began playing again.

The Adirondack kids looked around.

"Us?" Justin said.

The musician stopped playing and smiled. "That's right," he said, and pointed with his guitar pick. "There's no one here tonight yet except me and this

63

"There's no one here but me
and this gorgeous calico cat over here
on the rug," the musician said.

gorgeous calico cat over here on the rug. Do you like cats? She sure is a beauty." He began humming and strumming again.

"Dax!" Justin said. He ran toward the musician and there she was at the foot of the stage, sniffing a rug. "Jackie. Nick. Come here. You've got to see this."

"Funny thing about that bear skin rug," the guitar player said, as the Adirondack kids gathered in front of him. "Some nights when I play that rug is here and other nights it's gone – just vanished."

A young bus boy appeared from behind swinging kitchen doors. He hurried over to the guitar player and scooped up a dirty plate and glass. Hustling back toward the kitchen, Jackie called after him. "Excuse me," she said.

The bus boy froze, and slowly turned around. "Can I help you?" he said.

"Yes, you can," Jackie said. "I was just wondering." She paused. "Do you have any blueberry pie?"

Justin thought the bus boy looked nervous. Then he saw what Jackie saw. He motioned to Nick, whose eyes opened wide.

"They don't serve dinner here until 6 tonight," the bus boy said.

Jackie smiled. "I don't want dinner," she said. "I just wanted to know if you have any blueberry pie?"

The swinging kitchen doors burst open. "What's taking you so long to pick up one plate and a glass?" It was the dish washer. Then he saw the Adirondack kids. "Who are these guys?" he said.

The room went silent as the guitar player stopped playing, curious about the conversation unfolding in front of him.

"Well?" Jackie said. "Do you have any blueberry pie?"

The bus boy shook his head. "No," he said. "We don't have any blueberry pie."

Nick whispered to her. "You're not going to growl and jump on him, are you?" he said.

Jackie asked the bus boy one more time. "Are you sure you don't have any blueberry pie?" she said.

"I'm sure," the bus boy said.

"Then what's that I see all over your sneaker?" Jackie said.

"It looks like blueberry to me," Justin said.

Dax began wrestling with the leg of the bear skin rug.

"What's that Dax has wrapped around her paw?" Jackie said.

Justin knelt down to investigate. "It looks like a piece of string," he said.

"It is," Nick said. "It's my kite string!"

Jackie turned and smiled at the bus boy. "My name is Jackie," she said, and stretched out her hand. "And let me guess. You must be – the Labor Day Bear!"

epilogue

Justin backed his Adirondack chair away from the campfire that was roaring hot in the chilly mountain air. Propping his feet up on a log and settling in for a clear view of the fireworks soon to blaze across the ever darkening sky, he wondered at the day's events. Everything was still a blur, and in the quiet of the evening he could begin to sort things out.

His bucket hat was all the way down in the State of Delaware, but there was good news. Not only had the mystery of the Labor Day Bear finally been solved, but Ranger Bill had called. The Brown Pelican had been captured in time and would live!

And there would be no good-byes tonight. Because there had been so much extra activity throughout the day, his parents had decided to extend their stay. Before putting the *Tamarack* up in the boathouse for the season, he would get one more chance at his laker!

He watched and smiled as Jackie and Nick talked and laughed, their faces glowing orange in the flickering light. Dax jumped from the shadows into his lap and purred.

The first firework whistled through the air and lit up the sky, bursting into streams of red and white and blue. Was there any better place on the face of the earth to spend an entire summer?

There might be.

But Justin didn't think so.

DAX FACTS

Birds in the Adirondacks

Begin your own 'Life List.'' More than 200 different bird species can be found in the six-million acre Adirondack Park. Most birds breed in Spring and early Summer, but several do in Autumn (Cedar Waxwing and American Goldfinch) and even in late Winter (Great-horned Owl).

The best time to observe birds is in the early morning when they are most active. You can attract birds to your own backyard by providing plenty of food, shelter and water.

When you see one of the birds on the list that follows, check it! A good field guide with drawings or photographs and descriptions of birds will help greatly in accurate identification! Consider also writing down the date and location of the sightings.

Birding is enjoyed by millions of Americans, and is a hobby second only to gardening in popularity!

Short-eared Owl

OWLS
- [ ] Barred Owl
- [ ] Boreal Owl
- [ ] Eastern Screech Owl
- [ ] Great Gray Owl
- [ ] Great Horned Owl
- [ ] Hawk-owl
- [ ] Long-eared Owl
- [ ] Northern Saw-whet Owl
- [ ] Short-eared Owl
- [ ] Snowy Owl

PERCHING BIRDS
- [ ] Alder Flycatcher
- [ ] American Crow
- [ ] American Goldfinch
- [ ] American Redstart
- [ ] American Robin
- [ ] Belted Kingfisher
- [ ] Black & White Warbler
- [ ] Black-billed Cuckoo
- [ ] Blackburnian Warbler

- [ ] Black-capped Chickadee
- [ ] Black-throated Blue Warbler
- [ ] Black-throated Green Warbler
- [ ] Blue Jay
- [ ] Bobolink
- [ ] Bohemian Waxwing
- [ ] Boreal Chickadee
- [ ] Brown Creeper
- [ ] Brown-headed Cowbird
- [ ] Brown Thrasher
- [ ] Canada Warbler
- [ ] Cape May Warbler
- [ ] Cardinal
- [ ] Catbird
- [ ] Cedar Waxwing
- [ ] Chestnut-sided Warbler
- [ ] Chipping Sparrow
- [ ] Common Grackle
- [ ] Common Nighthawk
- [ ] Common Raven
- [ ] Common Redpoll

Common Yellowthroat

- [ ] Common Yellowthroat
- [ ] Dark-eyed Junco
- [ ] Eastern Bluebird

- [ ] Eastern Kingbird
- [ ] Eastern Meadowlark
- [ ] Eastern Phoebe
- [ ] Eastern Wood Phoebe
- [ ] European Starling
- [ ] Evening Grosbeak
- [ ] Field Sparrow
- [ ] Fox Sparrow
- [ ] Golden-crowned Kinglet
- [ ] Grasshopper Sparrow
- [ ] Gray Cheeked Thrush
- [ ] Gray Jay
- [ ] Great Crested Flycatcher

Hermit Thrush

- [ ] Hermit Thrush
- [ ] Hoary Redpoll
- [ ] Horned Lark
- [ ] House Finch
- [ ] House Sparrow
- [ ] House Wren
- [ ] Indigo Bunting
- [ ] Lapland Longspur
- [ ] Least Flycatcher
- [ ] Loggerhead Shrike
- [ ] Long-billed Marsh Wren
- [ ] Magnolia Warbler

- [ ] Mockingbird
- [ ] Mourning Warbler
- [ ] Nashville Warbler
- [ ] Northern Oriole
- [ ] Northern Parula
- [ ] Northern Shrike
- [ ] Northern Waterthrush
- [ ] Olive-sided Flycatcher
- [ ] Ovenbird
- [ ] Pine Grosbeak
- [ ] Pine Siskin
- [ ] Pine Warbler
- [ ] Purple Finch
- [ ] Red-breasted Nuthatch
- [ ] Red Crossbill
- [ ] Red-eyed Vireo
- [ ] Red-winged Blackbird
- [ ] Rose-breasted Grosbeak
- [ ] Ruby-crowned Kinglet
- [ ] Ruby-throated Hummingbird
- [ ] Rufous-sided Towee
- [ ] Rusty Blackbird
- [ ] Savannah Sparrow
- [ ] Scarlet Tanager
- [ ] Short-billed Marsh Wren
- [ ] Song Sparrow
- [ ] Snow Bunting
- [ ] Solitary Vireo
- [ ] Swainson's Thrush
- [ ] Swamp Sparrow
- [ ] Tree Sparrow
- [ ] Tufted Titmouse
- [ ] Veery
- [ ] Vesper Sparrow
- [ ] Warbling Vireo

- ❑ Whip-poor-will
- ❑ White-breasted Nuthatch
- ❑ White-crowned Sparrrow
- ❑ White-throated Sparrow
- ❑ White-winged Crossbill
- ❑ Willow Flycatcher
- ❑ Winter Wren
- ❑ Wood Thrush
- ❑ Yellow-bellied Flycatcher
- ❑ Yellow-billed Cuckoo
- ❑ Yellow-rumped Warbler
- ❑ Yellow-throated Vireo
- ❑ Yellow Warbler

PREY, BIRDS OF
- ❑ American Kestral
- ❑ Bald Eagle
- ❑ Black Vulture
- ❑ Broad-winged Hawk
- ❑ Cooper's Hawk
- ❑ Golden Eagle
- ❑ Gyrfalcon
- ❑ Marsh Hawk
- ❑ Merlin
- ❑ Northern Goshawk

Osprey

- ❑ Osprey
- ❑ Peregrine Falcon

- ❑ Red-tailed Hawk
- ❑ Red-shouldered Hawk
- ❑ Rough-legged Hawk
- ❑ Sharp-shinned Hawk
- ❑ Turkey Vulture

SHORE & WATER, BIRDS OF
- ❑ American Bittern
- ❑ American Coot
- ❑ Black-crowned Night-Heron
- ❑ Black Tern
- ❑ Cattle Egret
- ❑ Common Loon
- ❑ Common Moorhen
- ❑ Common Tern
- ❑ Double-crested Cormorant
- ❑ Glossy Ibis
- ❑ Great Blue Heron
- ❑ Great Egret
- ❑ Green-backed Heron
- ❑ Herring Gull
- ❑ Horned Grebe
- ❑ Killdeer
- ❑ King Rail
- ❑ Least Bittern
- ❑ Little Blue Heron
- ❑ Pied-billed Grebe
- ❑ Ring-billed Gull
- ❑ Sanderling
- ❑ Semipalmated Plover
- ❑ Sora
- ❑ Spotted Sandpiper
- ❑ Upland Plover

- ❏ Virginia Rail
- ❏ Yellow-crowned Night-Heron

SWIFTS & SWALLOWS
- ❏ Bank Swallow
- ❏ Barn Swallow
- ❏ Chimney Swift
- ❏ Cliff Swallow
- ❏ Northern Rough-winged Swallow
- ❏ Purple Martin

Common Snipe

Tree Swallow

- ❏ Tree Swallow

UPLAND GAME BIRDS
- ❏ American Woodcock
- ❏ Common Snipe
- ❏ Great Patridge
- ❏ Green Pheasant

- ❏ Mourning Dove
- ❏ Ring-necked Pheasant
- ❏ Rock Dove
- ❏ Ruffed Grouse
- ❏ Spruced Grouse
- ❏ Wild Turkey

WATERFOWL
- ❏ American Widgeon
- ❏ Barrow's Goldeneye
- ❏ Blue-winged Teal
- ❏ Brant
- ❏ Bufflehead
- ❏ Canada Goose
- ❏ Canvasback
- ❏ Common Eider
- ❏ Common Goldeneye
- ❏ Common Merganser
- ❏ Gadwall
- ❏ Greater Scaup
- ❏ Green-winged Teal
- ❏ Hooded Merganser

- Lesser Scaup
- Mallard
- Mute Swan
- Northern Pintail
- Northern Shoveler
- Oldsquaw
- Red-breasted Merganser
- Redhead
- Ring-necked Duck
- Ruddy Duck
- Snow Goose
- Tundra Swan
- Wood Duck

- Pileated Woodpecker
- Red-headed Woodpecker
- Three-toed Woodpecker
- Yellow-bellied Sapsucker

Red-breasted Mergansers

WOODPECKERS

- Black-backed Woodpecker
- Common Flicker
- Downy Woodpecker
- Hairy Woodpecker

*List compiled from *Birds of the Adirondacks – A Field Guide*, published by North Country Books, Utica, New York

Black-backed Woodpecker

Mallards

 DAX FACTS

Brown Pelican and Double-Crested Cormorant

In August of 2009, a **Brown Pelican** made an unexpected visit to the Adirondack Park. While the western American White Pelican has been known to make very rare appearances in the Adirondacks,

this was believed to have been the first visit by the Brown Pelican, which is normally found gliding along southern seashores.

It is still a mystery how this Brown Pelican made its way into the Adirondacks, but upon capture was discovered to be ill.

It is easy to understand in the story, *The Final Daze of Summer*, how Jackie confused the description given by Nick of the rare pelican with the local **Double-crested Cormorant**, which is also darkish in color and has a long hooked bill.

Those who come upon a sick or injured bird should not touch it, but notify authorities such as officials from the U.S. Fish & Wildlife Service, the Department of Environmental Conservation (DEC) or a local licensed rehabilitator, who will evaluate the situation and coordinate any attempts at rescue.

Above: **Double-crested Cormorant photographed at Fourth Lake in the Adirondacks.** *Photograph ® Gary Allen VanRiper*

Opposite: **Brown Pelican photographed on Fourth Lake in the Adirondack Park.** *Photograph by Carolyn Bernap, used by permission*

 **DAX FACTS**

The Adirondack Park

The Adirondack Park was established in 1892 by the State of New York. It's 6.1 million acres makes the Park the size of the neighboring state of Vermont, or larger in size than the Everglades, Yellowstone, Glacier and Grand Canyon National Park... COMBINED!

The summit of Mount Marcy. *Photograph ® Gary Allen VanRiper*

Sign welcoming visitors to the Adirondack Park. ®*Gary Allen VanRiper*

More than 55 different species of mammals can be found in the Adirondacks, and more than 200 species of birds. More than 2,000 miles of hiking trails gives millions of annual visitors intimate access to the many miles of rivers and streams and the many lakes and ponds and mountains – including access to the highest point in New York state – at 5,343 feet – Mount Marcy.

PBS Television has produced a wonderful program entitled, *The Adirondacks*, now available on home video.

Above: **Dawn on Raquette Lake.** Photograph ® Gary Allen VanRiper

Opposite: **White-tailed Deer.** Photograph ® Gary Allen VanRiper

About the Authors

Gary and Justin VanRiper are a father-and-son writing team residing with their family and cat, Dax, in Camden, New York. They spend many summer and autumn days at camp on Fourth Lake in the Adirondacks.

The Adirondack Kids® began as a writing exercise at home when Justin was in third grade. Encouraged after a public reading of the piece at a Parents As Reading Partners (PARP) event at school, the project grew into a middle-reader chapter book series.

The fifth book in the *The Adirondack Kids®* series, *Islands in the Sky*, won the 2005–06 Adirondack Literary Award for Best Children's Book. Books in the series are used in schools throughout the state of New York and titles also regularly appear on the New York State Charlotte Award's Suggested Reading List. To date, some 100,000 of *The Adirondack Kids®* books have been sold.

The authors often visit elementary schools, libraries and conferences to inspire and encourage young people to read and write.

The Adirondack Kids® writing and illustrating team. From left:
Gary, Carol and Justin VanRiper. *Photograph © Adirondack Kids Press, Ltd.*

About the Illustrators

Carol McCurn VanRiper lives and works in Camden, New York. She is also the wife and mother, respectively, of *The Adirondack Kids*® co-authors, Gary and Justin VanRiper. She inherited the job as publicist when *The Adirondack Kids*® grew from a dream to a small family business. Her interior black-and-white illustrations appear in *The Adirondack Kids*® books, #4 – #10.

Susan Loeffler is a freelance illustrator who lives in Central New York. Her full-color cover illustrations appear on every book in *The Adirondack Kids*® series, including on the cover of *The Adirondack Kids*® coloring book, *Runaway Dax*, which also features her interior black-and-white illustrations.

ᵀʰᵉ**Adirondack Kids**® #1

Justin Robert is ten years old and likes computers, biking and peanut butter cups. But his passion is animals. When an uncommon pair of Common Loons takes up residence on Fourth Lake near the family camp, he will do anything he can to protect them.

ᵀʰᵉ**Adirondack Kids**® #2
Rescue on Bald Mountain

Justin Robert and Jackie Salsberry are on a special mission. It is Fourth of July weekend in the Adirondacks and time for the annual ping-pong ball drop at Inlet. Their best friend, Nick Barnes, has won the opportunity to release the balls from a seaplane, but there is just one problem. He is afraid of heights. With a single day remaining before the big event, Justin and Jackie decide there is only one way to help Nick overcome his fear. Climb Bald Mountain!

ᵀʰᵉ**Adirondack Kids**® #3
The Lost Lighthouse

Justin Robert, Jackie Salsberry and Nick Barnes are fishing under sunny Adirondack skies when a sudden and violent storm chases them off Fourth Lake and into an unfamiliar forest – a forest that has harbored a secret for more than 100 years.

The Adirondack Kids® #4
The Great Train Robbery

It's all aboard the train at the North Creek station, and word is out there are bandits in the region. Will the train be robbed? Justin Robert and Jackie Salsberry are excited. Nick Barnes is bored – but he won't be for long.

The Adirondack Kids® #5
Islands in the Sky

Justin Robert, Jackie Salsberry and Nick Barnes head for the Adirondack high peaks wilderness – while Justin's calico cat, Dax, embarks on an unexpected tour of the Adirondack Park.

The Adirondack Kids® #6
Secret of the Skeleton Key

While preparing their pirate ship for the Anything That Floats Race, Justin and Nick discover an antique bottle riding the waves on Fourth Lake. Inside the bottle is a key that leads The Adirondack Kids to unlock an old camp mystery.

Also available on **The Adirondack Kids®** official web site
www.ADIRONDACKKIDS.com
Watch for more adventures of The Adirondack Kids® coming soon.

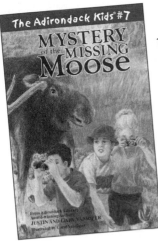

The Adirondack Kids® #7
Mystery of the Missing Moose

Justin Robert has the camera. Nick Barnes has the binoculars. And Jackie Salsberry has the common sense! The Adirondack Kids are led into a series of unexpected encounters with local wildlife as they search Eagle Bay for any sign of a missing moose!

The Adirondack Kids® #8
Escape from Black Bear Mountain

Justin Robert wants to climb all of the mountains near his family's Fourth Lake camp before the summer is over. Jackie Salsberry can't wait to join him. Nick Barnes would rather go fishing. Next on the list is Black Bear Mountain. An easy hike, right? If only they had noticed the "trail closed" sign before they took off together.

Over
100,000
Adirondack Kids
BOOKS
SOLD!

The Adirondack Kids® #9
Legend of the Lake Monster

For more than 400 years, hundreds of people have claimed to have seen a strange creature in Lake Champlain. Is there anything mysterious lurking in those deep waters? Join best friends Justin Robert, Jackie Salsberry and Nick Barnes – The Adirondack Kids – on their quest for the answer.

Watch for more adventures
of The Adirondack Kids® coming soon.